TOO PRINCESSY!

To Gina and Stephanie—
the original princesses
—J. R.

To Charles, who has turned
so many boxes into castles
—G. L.

ISBN 978-0-545-47274-6

12 11 10 9 8 7 6 5 4 3 2 1 12 13 14 15 16 17/0

Printed in the U.S.A. 08

First Scholastic printing, October 2012

Art created in Adobe Illustrator
Typeset in Keener
Book design by Geneviève Leloup

TOO PRINCESSY!

JEAN REIDY

ILLUSTRATED BY

GENEVIÈVE LELOUP

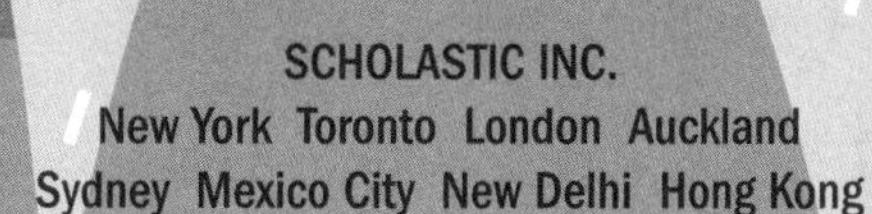

SCHOLASTIC INC.
New York Toronto London Auckland
Sydney Mexico City New Delhi Hong Kong

TOYS

I AM BORED!

TOO JOLLY
TOO JUMPY,
TOYS

TOO DIGGY, TOO D MPY!

TOO PIECEY,

TOO BLINKY,

TOYS
TOO BANGY,

TOO PLINKY.

TOO GOOPY,

TOO GLUEY,

TOO
MARSY,

TOO MOOEY!

TOO FUZZY,

TOO SLEEPY,

TOO CRAWLY, TOO CREEPY.

TOO SOAPY,

TOO SPRINGY,

TOO

ZOOMY...

TOO RINGY.

TOO CIRCUSY,
TOYS
TOO CLOWNY,

TOO PRINCESSY!

TOO CROWNY.

SO...
TOYS

...FUN! LET'S PLAY.

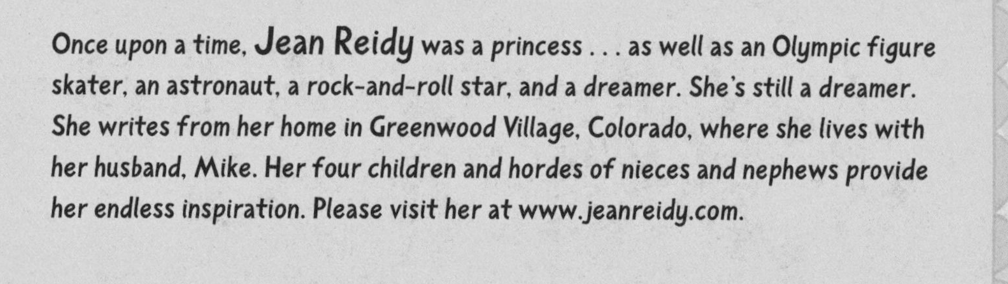

Once upon a time, **Jean Reidy** was a *princess* . . . as well as an Olympic figure skater, an astronaut, a *rock-and-roll star*, and a *dreamer*. She's still a *dreamer*. She writes from her home in Greenwood Village, Colorado, where she lives with her husband, Mike. Her four children and hordes of nieces and nephews provide her endless inspiration. Please visit her at www.jeanreidy.com.

Geneviève Leloup studied graphic arts, animation, and printing in Belgium, where she was born. Her whimsical illustrations have appeared in magazines and on various products, including lots of textiles and children's clothing. When not drawing or traveling, she bakes large amounts of cookies and plays accordion in her Brooklyn digs. You can visit her at www.alulustudio.com.